# MR. CHEEKY

by Roger Hargreaves

D0318316

EGMONT

**MR.MEN**　**LITTLE MISS**

MR. MEN and LITTLE MISS™& © The Hargreaves Organisation

Mr. Cheeky copyright © 2001 The Hargreaves Organisation
Printed and published under licence from Price Stern Sloan Inc., Los Angeles.

The character and design of Mr. Cheeky was devised by
Gemma Almond, aged 8, from Shropshire

First published in Great Britain 2001
This edition published in Great Britain 2005
by Egmont Books Limited
239 Kensington High Street, London W8 6SA

ISBN 0 7498 5457 X
11 13 15 17 19 20 18 16 14 12
Printed in the UK

# MR. CHEEKY

Inspired by
**Gemma Almond**

Written and illustrated by
**Adam Hargreaves**

# Who is MR. CHEEKY?

The Mr Men & Little Miss are 30 years old and to celebrate their birthday we launched a children's competition to create a new Mr Man or Little Miss character.

And here is the winner – Mr Cheeky!

This is the first new Mr Man to be published since 1988. My father created over 70 Mr Men & Little Miss during the 1970s and 80s. We thought it would be fun if one of the millions of children that read and love the Mr Men were to create a new character.

Gemma Almond, aged eight from Shropshire, was one of the children to enter the competition. Gemma came up with the idea of Mr Cheeky.

All children are a little bit cheeky at times, so I thought it was the perfect name for a new Mr Man. I also thought her drawing of Mr Cheeky had all the right ingredients – a simple shape, bright colours and a little blue hat.

I have taken Gemma's idea and written and illustrated this book all about Mr Cheeky. I hope you enjoy it.

**CHILDREN with LEUKAEMIA**
Registered Charity No. 298405

When Paul O'Gorman died of leukaemia in February 1987, aged fourteen,
he made his parents promise to help other children with leukaemia.
It was a promise they were able to keep with the active support of Diana,
Princess of Wales, who inaugurated the charity
CHILDREN with LEUKAEMIA in January 1988.

A courageous, fun-loving boy who never gave up hope,
Paul's indomitable spirit inspires the work of CHILDREN with LEUKAEMIA.
In a few short years it has grown to be the leading charity dedicated
exclusively to the conquest of childhood leukaemia through research
and treatment and to the welfare of leukaemic children and their families.

CHILDREN with LEUKAEMIA will not rest until childhood leukaemia
becomes a disease of the past and no family need suffer in the
way that the O'Gormans and other families have.

*For further information contact:*
CHILDREN with LEUKAEMIA, 51 Great Ormond Street, London WC1N 3JQ
Tel: 020 7404 0808 Fax: 020 7404 3666 www.leukaemia.org

Mr Greedy was sitting down at his kitchen table having breakfast – cornflakes, toast, eggs, butter, marmalade, milk, sugar, more toast – when there was a knock at the door.

As he opened it somebody barged past him.

That somebody sat down and poured some of Mr Greedy's cornflakes into Mr Greedy's bowl.

Mr Greedy didn't know what to say.

The somebody ate the cornflakes.

Then the somebody ate the toast, the eggs, the butter, the marmalade, milk and sugar, and got up to go.

"Thanks, Tubby!" laughed the somebody as he walked out of the door.

Mr Greedy just couldn't believe what had happened. His breakfast! All gone!

Now, you would have to agree that somebody who could do that would have to be very cheeky, the cheekiest somebody in the world.

Mr Cheeky.

Mr Cheeky walked down the lane from Mr Greedy's house with a wide grin on his face. He was enjoying himself.

And he continued to enjoy himself for the rest of the day.

Further along the lane Mr Cheeky met Little Miss Neat, who was painting her fence.
"Do you want to do some painting?" asked Little Miss Neat.

Mr Cheeky picked up a spare paintbrush and painted over Little Miss Neat's glasses.

"Thanks, Four Eyes!" he laughed.
Little Miss Neat was lost for words.

Just outside Town Mr Cheeky met Mr Nosey.
Mr Nosey had hurt the end of his nose.

"Could you help me bandage my nose?" he asked.
"Do it yourself, Big Nose," laughed Mr Cheeky.

Mr Nosey was lost for words.

Mr Cheeky walked into Town and went into
the bakers.
He walked straight to the front of the queue.

"Excuse me," said Mr Small, who was next in line,
"There's a queue here!"
"And I'm at the front of it, Shorty," laughed
Mr Cheeky and stuck his tongue out.

Mr Small was lost for words.

Mr Cheeky walked out feeling very pleased with
himself.

Mr Muddle asked him for directions to the greengrocer to buy some toothpaste. Mr Cheeky told him to get lost...
and Mr Muddle did.

That evening while out for a walk, Little Miss Neat met Mr Greedy and Mr Muddle.

"Mr Cheeky needs to be taught a lesson!" said Little Miss Neat.
"I agree," said Mr Greedy.
"I disagree," said Mr Muddle, who was as muddled as usual.
"And I know just the person to teach him that lesson," said Little Miss Neat.

Very early the next morning, Mr Cheeky was awoken by a knock at his door.

It was Little Miss Bossy.

"I've come to stay," announced Little Miss Bossy.
"But…" began Mr Cheeky.
"No buts, and I'd like my breakfast. Right away," ordered Little Miss Bossy.
"Get it yourself!" said Mr Cheeky.
"WRONG! BREAKFAST! NOW! PLEASE!" yelled Little Miss Bossy.

Mr Cheeky was lost for words.

Mr Cheeky was so stunned that he actually did as he was told.

After breakfast, he decided to go for a walk. He wasn't enjoying Little Miss Bossy's company very much.

"Don't forget the washing up," cried Little Miss Bossy.
"Do it yourself!" said Mr Cheeky.
"WRONG! WASHING UP! NOW! PLEASE!" ordered Little Miss Bossy.

Mr Cheeky washed up.

After washing up, Mr Cheeky tried to creep out through the back door.

"Where do you think you're going?" cried Little Miss Bossy. "The lawn needs cutting," she said.
"Cut it yourself!" said Mr Cheeky.
"WRONG! LAWN! CUT! NOW! PLEASE!" ordered Little Miss Bossy.

Mr Cheeky cut the lawn.

And so it continued all week long. Every time Mr Cheeky opened his mouth or tried to sneak away, there was Little Miss Bossy shouting,
"WRONG!"
"WRONG!"
"WRONG!"

At the end of a very tiring week, it was a very miserable Mr Cheeky who answered the door when Mr Greedy and Little Miss Neat visited.

It was also a very polite Mr Cheeky.

He made them tea.
He offered them biscuits. Mr Greedy ate five.
And he didn't call Mr Greedy Tubby.
And he didn't call Little Miss Neat Four Eyes.

"Well, I think it's worked," announced Little Miss Neat.

"He's a changed person," agreed Mr Greedy.

"I think you can go home now, Little Miss Bossy."

"That's a shame," she replied, "I was really enjoying myself."

Mr Cheeky showed them to the door.
"And remember," said Little Miss Bossy, "Any more
of your cheek and I shall be round to stay again."
Mr Cheeky closed the door. And then very softly,
under his breath, he said,
"bossy boots."

The door sprang open.

"THAT'S... RIGHT!" cried Little Miss Bossy and went home chuckling to herself.